A Midsummer Foy

Janice Armstrong & Meilo So

So & Co books

Text copyright 2011 by Janice Armstrong
Illustrations copyright 2011 by Meilo So
All rights reserved
Published in the United Kingdom by
So & Co Books
www.bluemull.com

A Midsummer Foy
ISBN 978-0-9563049-1-9

Produced In Hong Kong
By MI Design Ltd
March 2011
First Edition

I, Vaila
have a tale to tell,
turn the pages
and listen well.

John Ross, Ingrid,
Magnus and me
went fishing
out on a silky sea.
Down went the lines
to the liquid black
and up came
mackerel, haddock and brill
and the basket filled
and the water licked
the cup and curve
of our boat.

So we never saw
the fog
gliding over
the milky sea.
Without a sound
it wrapped us round
and I shivered
and reached for
Ingrid's hand.

Then Magnus spoke,
"The sea is breathing"
and suddenly
dorsal fins
like black scythes
sliced the water.

Our boat rocked
as the giants
tumbled round,
but wood is no food
for a whale
so they passed
and were lost
in the Sound.

At last we saw
a smudge of
darker grey
and made our way
to land.

Safely tied,
we spied a path
and up we climbed,
but something moved
and breathed close by,
something tickled my spine.

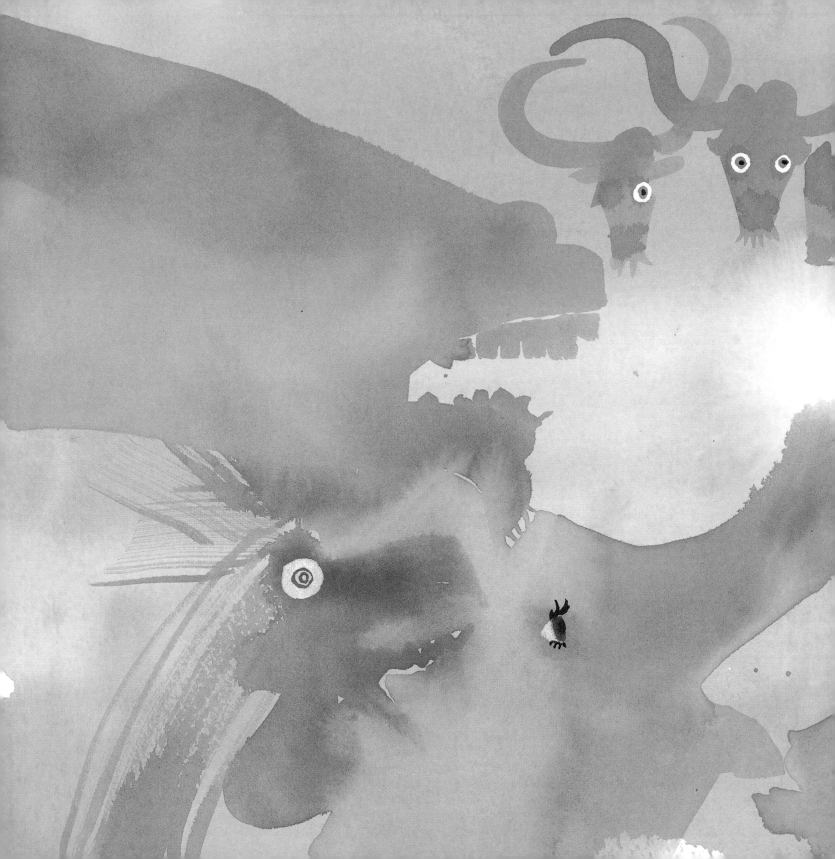

I held my breath,
my ears throbbed,
I strained to hear a sound.
Only the drift of the mist
so I turned to carry on.

"Ingrid, Magnus,
John Ross!"
But my voice fell
flat in the fog.

I stumbled over stones
and splashed in mud,
a whinny,
thud,
a clap and flap of wings,
shadows formed
then drained to white again.
"Magnus, Ingrid,
John Ross!"
I called and called again.
And then at last
a muffled voice,
"Vaila! This way!
See what we have found!"

I followed the voices
through the gloom
and found them by
a massive wall of stone.

Our fingers trailed
the cold damp walls
until we reached two heavy
wooden doors.
Together we pushed
and entered
a massive hall.

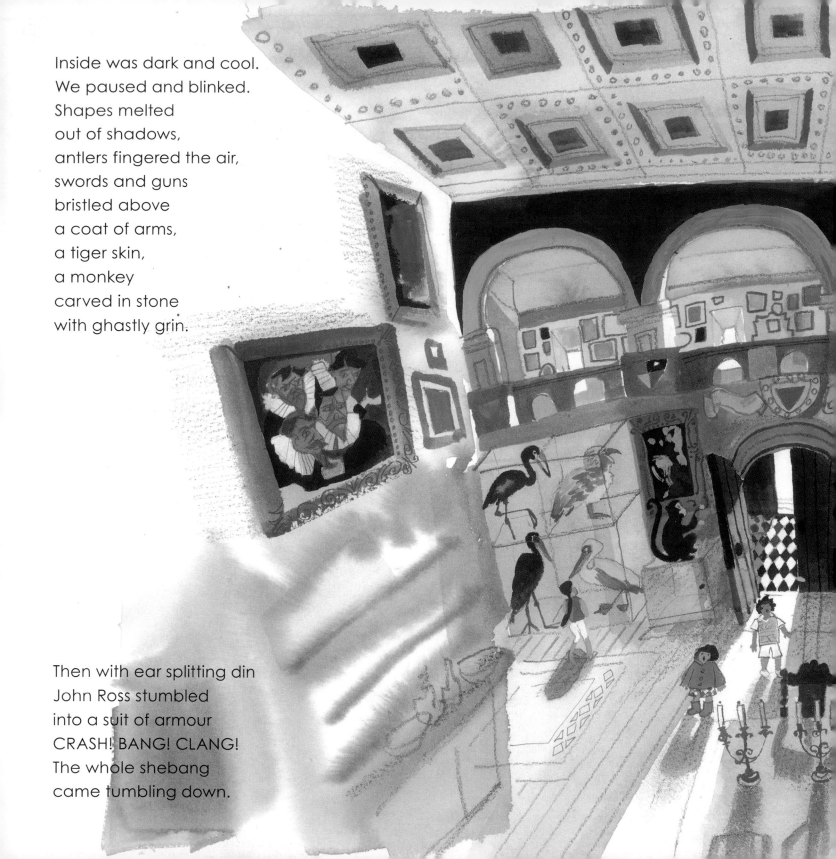

Inside was dark and cool.
We paused and blinked.
Shapes melted
out of shadows,
antlers fingered the air,
swords and guns
bristled above
a coat of arms,
a tiger skin,
a monkey
carved in stone
with ghastly grin.

Then with ear splitting din
John Ross stumbled
into a suit of armour
CRASH! BANG! CLANG!
The whole shebang
came tumbling down.

Then
a bark!
A voice outside.
HIDE!
We dived
under the table.
O no!
O please!
I squeezed
myself small
to nothing at all.

First came a dog,
tongue lolling,
then hairy boots,
a flowery skirt
and a woman's voice
calling,

"You clumsy dog!
Come here at once!
I'll turn
you into
doggy chunks!"

Huddled close
we heard
Chzzz! Chzzz!
of a knife
being sharpened,
chopping,
banging,
pans rattling,
a voice humming.

"Be still
my hairy friend!"
the lilting voice
commanded
and a knife
came thudding down.
I cried aloud
and tears
rolled down my cheeks,
when suddenly I felt
a warm wet tongue
lick them clean.

A face appeared,
bright and curious,
"What have we here?
More stew for the pot?"

The game was up.
We all crawled out
and followed her into
a kitchen
bright and warm.
She cut some cake
and put the kettle on.
Her name was Olga,
and as we told our tale
she licked her fingers,
smiled and said,
"With all this fog
you'll have to stay.

Tonight it is
the summer foy.
I have a banquet
to prepare.
There's lots to do,
so roll your sleeves up
you can help too!"

Into a truck
we scrambled
and bounced
a bumpy road
to the pigs.
"Slip slop
my little
sausages!"
she called
and poured
a rich broth
of peelings and cuttings
into their trough.

Then to the hens
who eyed us
suspiciously,
as we gathered
their eggs.

On to the garden
we trooped,
and in showers
of peaty earth
pulled carrots
and beetroot
up to the light.

Baskets of berries
spilled into
hungry mouths,
and warm in the sun,
red lipped
and purple tongued
I began to doze.

Back in the kitchen
among the
steaming pans,
we filleted
and boned,
fish scales
on hot cheeks,
silver on our hands.

Olga tied
an apron
round my waist
and I began to bake,
floury bannocks
and chocolate cake,
whilst she
made sausages,
string after string,
"A family recipe"
she said with a grin.

Soon the hall
began to fill with
rich and lovely smells.

Roast chicken
and raspberry fool,
pig on a spit,
guacamole,
summer berries
and honey cakes,
lamb kebabs
and sirloin steaks,
toffee apples,
crispy strudel,
blueberry tart
and black
squid noodle.

Then over the hill
in the soft summer sun,
music drifted,
a horse and cart
rumbled,
acrobats tumbled,
women twirling,
skirts birling,
all the colours
of summer.

Olga ran out
to welcome them in
and soon the hall filled
with the merriest din.

Jugs of sweet juices,
our cups overflowed,
speeches were made,
stories were told
and the food!
Oh! The food never ended,
dish after dish,
from lemon meringue
to our succulent fish.

Then fiddles
flew in a frenzy
of sound,
lifting our feet
to dance
quadrilles and lancers
under the midnight sun.

And John Ross,
Ingrid, Magnus
and me
joined the ring
and the skylark
vied with the violin
and in the centre
of us all,
Olga,
in shining dress
blue like a summer sea,
twirled and spun
laughed and sang.

When they left,
I do not know,
but slowly
I lifted
leg after leg
and climbed,
yawning,
into a canopied bed,
garlanded drapes
falling round my head.
Olga tucked me in
and said,
"Sweet dreams
little sausage!"

I dreamed
of whales
in party hats,
of pigs playing fiddles
and acrobats,
then swirling fog
wrapped me round
and I woke with a start,
to the smell
of bacon grilling
down below,
my mother calling,
the radio.
Shaking the dreams
from my tousled head,
I rose from
my bed
and smiled.

For Finley- JA
For Brian, Peter, Clare
&
Ron- MS

Special thanks to Dorota Rychlik
who inspired this tale

by Vaila

SO & CO BOOKS